One Potato, Two Potato

One Potato, Two Potato

Edited by Bernagh Brims

Illustrated by Duncan Smith

Appletree Press

First published in 1990 by the Appletree Press Ltd,
. 7 James Street South, Belfast BT2 8DL

The publisher gratefully acknowledges the
financial assistance of the Northern Bank Ltd

**British Library Cataloguing in Publication
Data**
Brims, Bernagh
One potato, two potato.
1. Children's short stories in English – Anthologies
I. Title II. Smith, Duncan *1957–*
823.01089282 [J]

ISBN 0-86281-258-5

Contents

NIALL OF THE NINE NOSES

Jennifer McCully

Have you ever wondered why County Armagh is called 'The Orchard of Ireland'? Well maybe this is why. The story begins, not in County Armagh at all, but right away up in the very north of County Antrim.

Up there, a long time ago, there lived a giant called Niall of the Nine Noses. Now, he didn't actually *have* nine noses, he just had the one, but it was so big it was about the same size as nine ordinary noses all rolled into one. He was the ugliest giant you could ever imagine and he lived in an enormous castle perched right on a cliff-top overlooking the sea.

Nothing grew up there, except for one tree which stood on a little patch of ground near Niall's castle. It was a most beautiful apple tree and Niall was very proud of it. No-one ever knew how Niall came to have such a wonderful tree, but he guarded it jealously, built a huge wall right round it, and no-one was ever allowed near it, either to look at it or pull any of the apples which hung on its boughs.

As time passed, word of the beautiful tree spread through the length and breadth of Ireland and people longed to see it and perhaps even get some of the fruit from its branches. A few tried, but no-one ever succeeded. They were all caught and kept prisoner by Niall of the Nine Noses and made to look after the beautiful tree, watering it, pruning it, putting manure round its roots. And every year the tree grew more and more beautiful.

Down in the heart of County Armagh, there lived two brothers – Con McDermott and his brother Red. Red's real name was Michael,

They were all caught and kept prisoner by Niall of the Nine Noses and made to look after the beautiful tree.

but because he always wore a little red feather sticking out of the top of his hat, everyone called him Red.

The brothers had heard of Niall's wonderful tree and they decided they should be the ones to get some of the apples. That is, Con decided. He also decided Red should be the one to go over the wall to get them.

'Yes, I've decided to let *you* have the honour of doin' it,' said Con one day. 'Just think how famous you'll be if – er – I mean *when* you manage it.'

'Huh – a fat lot of use that will be to me if I'm caught. Still, it's not right for that ugly big lump of a giant to be so greedy and keep all the apples to himself,' answered Red.

'Good man yourself,' shouted Con in glee, 'and that's why we're, I mean *you're* goin' to get some apples off him.'

'Ooo, I don't know about … ' began Red.

'Now quit bletherin' and come on,' interrupted Con. 'Here, what's that funny noise?'

'What noise might that be?' asked Red tremblingly.

'Ach man, are y'deaf?' answered Con. 'That sort of clatterin' and rattlin' noise?'

'Sure don't y'know rightly it's me teeth chatterin' and me knees knockin' together with the fright of thinkin' about that big, ugly brute with his big, ugly nose. I'll hardly have a tooth left in me head or a bone in me body by the time we get there,' babbled Red.

'I'm listenin' to no more of your nonsense,' said Con crossly. 'Off we go to the castle of Niall of the Nine Noses.'

After several days walking they arrived at their journey's end. There in front of them was the wall behind which grew the beautiful tree, and after much scraping and scrambling Con managed to heave Red far enough up for him to see over. But the terrible sight was too much for him.

'In the name o'glory Con, get me down quick – QUICK!'

There was a bump as he fell to the ground.

'He's there, he's there,' he gasped, as he lay puffing and wheezing on the ground. 'He's lyin' under the tree fast asleep. I could see his big ugly brute of a nose swayin' in the breeze – and – and – what's more, I'm not goin' over that wall.'

'Oh aren't you now,' said Con, and before Red knew what was happening, Con gave him a tremendous shove that landed him right over the wall onto the ground on the other side. Once there, Red wasn't sure *what* to do, but as he couldn't stay where he was and he couldn't climb back he thought he'd better try to get what he had come for. How was he to reach the apples with the giant lying asleep right under the tree?

Very quietly, he began to crawl up Niall's left leg to his shoulder and then started to creep across his chest to his other shoulder from where he hoped, if he stood on tiptoe, to be able to reach some of the apples which were hanging on the lower branches. But, just as he got half way across the giant's chest, what do you think happened? Well, his knees started to knock and his teeth to chatter and for the life of him he couldn't stop them.

'The stupid eejit,' said Con, who was watching from the top of the wall. 'That horrible racket's going to waken the giant up.'

And sure enough, it did. With a blood-curdling roar Niall woke up and grabbed a hold of Red in his big fist, and held him just below his huge nose. Poor Red shook and rattled harder then ever. He was sure that he was going to be eaten alive. He saw the giant's mouth open

He was sure that he was going to be eaten alive.

and he shut his eyes in terror. But suddenly, instead of biting him, Niall gave the most tremendous SNEEZE.

It was like a hurricane, a tornado, a cyclone, all in one. It blew Red right back over the wall and Con off the wall and they both landed in a heap on the other side.

'Wh-Wh-What happened?' asked Red in a dazed voice.

'Well – talk about a quare stroke of luck,' said Con. 'You know Niall grabbed a hold of you?'

'I don't think I'll ever forget it,' said Red weakly.

'Aye, well, just as he was holdin' you under that big nose of his you were shakin' an' rattlin' that hard that the feather in your hat started to shake too, and it tickled his nose and made him let that big ignorant sneeze out of him. And I'll tell you what's more – just look at the tree.'

Red looked – and he could hardly believe his eyes. There wasn't a single apple left on it. So great had been the sneeze of Niall of the Nine Noses, that he had blown every apple off the tree. It was as if the apples had been caught in a gale-force wind. They were blown the whole length of Ulster and ended up scattered all over County Armagh where the seeds took root and turned that county into 'The Orchard of Ireland'.

So next time you bite into a juicy apple dumpling just remember Niall of the Nine Noses and his beautiful tree and how, but for Con and Red, there might never have been any lovely Armagh apples for us to eat.

YELLOW WELLIES

Sam McBratney

It was what people call a lovely day outside when Colvin went into the garden wearing his new yellow wellies. High above his head, tiny white clouds drifted across the blue sky like puffs of smoke from a giant's pipe, and it was all very annoying, because Colvin wanted wet rain and lots of shiny puddles to walk in.

A head appeared above the hedge. This was Lisa, his good friend.

'I got new wellies,' Colvin said. 'Yellow wellies. I'm looking for a puddle in Johnston's field.'

'Yellow wellies,' said Lisa, stretching to look. 'I'd love a pair of yellow wellies. Yellow wellies, yellie wellows, wellow yellies ...' She gave up. 'It's not easy to say those two words when you say them fast.'

Colvin had never thought about the problem, so he had nothing to say about it. Lisa came with him across Johnston's field, which wasn't too easy to get through because of the head-high nettles and the prickly gorse. But it was worth it when they found a large, smooth puddle.

'Watch this,' said Colvin, and stepped in with both feet.

The puddle had a soft, slippery bottom. More than half of the yellow wellies disappeared under the water, which quickly turned muddy.

'Go in just a little bit further, Colvin,' said Lisa. 'It's not deep.'

Boldly leading with his left foot, Colvin took another step, and the cold water slurped over the top of his boot, filling it completely.

His sock, his ankle, his boot and all five of his toes were now under the muddy water.

Colvin got out of there quickly, but far too

The cold water slurped over the top of his boot, filling it completely.

late, of course. His left foot squelched. The puddle had won.

'Look what you made me do!' he said angrily to Lisa.

His Mummy was not pleased when Colvin walked through the door a few minutes later with his left foot squelching.

'In the name of goodness, Colvin, have you no wit! What is the point of me buying you new boots to keep your feet dry if you are going to use them to get your feet wet? How could you be so silly?'

'Mummy, I only wet one foot.'

'And that is one too many!'

With a nice dry pair of woollen socks on, Colvin went out to play again, this time in Lisa's garden, with Lisa and her fat old dog, Queenie. A man in dark clothes came round the corner of the house, and he was carrying a big sack of coal. Fat Dog Queenie paused long enough to wag her tail once in anger, then threw herself at the coalman's ankles with a rush.

'WUF WUF. RRRRAARRR.'

'Queenie!' Lisa was cross. 'Stop it, you bad dog, that's Mr Archbold with our coal. You are only supposed to bite *burglars*.'

'Here, girl,' said Mr Archbold, 'Come here till I see you, crosspatch, there's a good dog.'

'She's not good, thought Colvin, she's the worst dog in the whole street.' Fat Dog waddled up to the coalman and licked his black hands with her pink tongue.

'Ah! So she likes a bit of black stuff,' said Mr Archbold.

'Nothing likes soot, Mr Archbold,' Lisa said sensibly.

'Ah, now! You'd be surprised what eats what! Soot's the quare stuff!' And Mr Archbold tickled Queenie, aimed a wink at Colvin, and went away whistling like someone in a good mood.

An interesting question popped into Colvin's mind. Was it possible that Queenie ate soot? He'd certainly seen her trying to eat wasps buzzing round the bin. And she ate bits of stick. Fat Dog probably ate anything. He grabbed Queenie's food dish and disappeared with it into his own house, for he knew the very place to get some soot.

First he needed a spoon. The kitchen drawer! Then he scraped some soot from the back of his chimney into Fat Dog's dish. It looked a bit dry so he added some milk from a carton in the fridge.

'Is that you, Colvin?' said his mother's voice.

'No!' shouted Colvin, zooming through the back door with a bowlful of black goo.

He placed it under Queenie's nose.

'I don't want anything to do with this, Colvin,' warned Lisa. 'Nothing eats soot. It's rubbish.'

'No!' shouted Colvin, zooming through the
back door with a bowlful of black goo.

Fat Dog sniffed suspiciously at her dish, and instead of eating what was there, she walked right through it. The black stuff got stuck to her paws like paste. 'They are filthy!' Lisa cried in alarm.

The time had come, Queenie decided, for a proper game, so she jumped up on Lisa and her paws scored long, ugly black marks down the front of Lisa's lovely clean dress. Lisa's dark eyes glistened with fury and dismay. 'Look at what you have done to me, Colvin!' she shouted at him.

Colvin went home. He hid in the bathroom upstairs, but he knew he was doomed.

'*Col-vin!*' His Mummy called him down. A tortoise could have passed him as he came downstairs, and when he reached the back door Lisa's Mummy was there. This was what he had expected.

She'd brought Lisa's filthy dress and the dish

of soggy soot. And Lisa's Mummy was able to mention quite a few places inside the house where Queenie had planted her wet, black feet.

'I was going down town to buy shoes,' said Lisa, 'and now I can't go. I didn't get my shoes because of you, Colvin.'

A boring and miserable time now began for Colvin. His Mummy stuck him up in his room and told him to stay there until he'd had time to think about how to do good things instead of bad things. And all because of stupid Fat Dog! It was the yappiest thing on four legs and it deserved to be zapped for jumping up on people like that!

Time went by. Downstairs, Mrs Matthews was reading Colvin's baby brother a story on her knee when the living room door went 'Click'. Was that really Colvin standing there with Mr Moneypig under his arm? It was.

'Mummy, I don't want you to shout at me,'

he said quickly. 'I want to buy Lisa a present
and I want to use my money out of Mr
Moneypig.'

'What kind of present did you have in mind?'

'Something for her feet.'

Mrs Matthews listened carefully to what
Colvin had to say – and she thought that he'd
had a very good idea. 'All right, we'll use some

of your money to buy Lisa a present, and you can take it round to her after tea.'

'Great! People are going to like me again!' Colvin thought happily. 'And Lisa is going to be amazed!'

As soon as Colvin rapped Lisa's door after tea, Fat Dog started to bark and howl like a mad dog. Lisa spoke to Colvin through the letter-box.

'I'm not allowed to play with you, Colvin, and Queenie isn't allowed to play with you either.'

Good. He was never playing with Fat Dog again as long as he lived. He pushed his parcel against the letter-box so that Lisa could see it.

'I got a present for you. I thought of it all by myself, it was my idea.'

The letter-box snapped shut, and in a few seconds more Mrs Tomlinson opened the door. Lisa reached for the parcel immediately.

'I love presents. You have it really well wrapped up, Colvin. Oooo – in a box! I wonder what … Oh, Colvin! Yellow wellies!'

The smile on Colvin's face grew extraordinarily wide.

'It was my idea, I thought it up.'

'They are beautiful things!' cried Lisa, ripping off her shoes without bothering about the laces, and Colvin said, 'They are the same colour as Slippy Duck's beak, you know.'

'Whose beak?' asked Mrs Tomlinson.

'Slippy Duck, Mummy. He lives in Colvin's bath. Colvin, will you walk over to the puddle with me tomorrow?'

'I hope it rains all night!' Colvin shouted as he ran back home.

THE NUMBER NINE BUS

Bernard MacLaverty

Once upon a time there was a bus, Number Nine, who had worked all his days in a big city. It was an old bus and every time it came to a stop its brakes gave a long squeal which set the passengers' teeth on edge. When it came to a stop it shook and rattled and trembled all over. Even its bell was not working properly – instead of ringing it made a clunk sound, and nobody ever took the trouble to fix it.

One night when Number Nine was put into the garage and everyone had gone away he sighed to himself.

'Oh, I'm so tired. I'm getting old. I'll never be able to work in the morning. I wish they would give me a new set of tyres, my wheels are killing me.'

It was terrible; everything he hated happened to him that day.

But the next morning Number Nine had to go out like all the other buses. It was terrible; everything he hated happened to him that day.

For a start the driver was grumpy and bad tempered and shouted about how awful a bus Number Nine was. It was raining and the road was full of puddles and Number Nine coughed and spluttered in the fumes of the other cars when he had to wait in traffic jams.

When people got on the bus they were soaking wet. Their umbrellas dripped and his windows steamed up so much he could hardly see where he was going. He could feel himself rusting in the damp. Mud splashed up over his blue and cream paint.

'What a day,' he said. 'Will it ever be over?'

But still it went on. That night some boys got on the bus and wrote on the walls with felt-tipped pens. 'Billy loves Rosemary' and 'Rosemary loves Billy'. They tore some of the seats, they shouted and laughed and jumped off without paying any money. Number Nine limped home and when the garage was quiet he said to himself:

'Whatever will I do? I'm so tired. I'm getting old. I'll never be able to work in the morning.'

This time he was right. In the cold of the morning Number Nine could not start and he was left to rest for the day.

In the middle of the afternoon he heard some voices and footsteps. It was the chief inspector and a woman. The woman was young and nice. She said, 'Yes, I think this one will do.'

'What is going to happen to me now,' thought Number Nine. 'Are they going to send me to the scrap yard?'

The woman got into the bus and because she spoke kindly it started first time.

'Come along old bus. You can make it up this hill,' she said. The woman drove the bus away from the city to a place Number Nine had never seen before. The roads were not crowded with other cars. There were green fields and trees and flowers. Number Nine began to feel happy.

'This is better than work,' he said.

He was put in a warm garage that night and the next day a lot of people began painting him different bright colours. Blue and red and yellow and green; and they drew pictures of animals all over him until Number Nine thought he must be the nicest looking bus in the world. They painted big letters on his side which said 'Playbus'. A man came and fixed his brakes so that they didn't squeal and set the children's teeth on edge. He put new tyres on and stopped him rattling. And best of all he fixed his bell so that it pinged clearly.

The next day the nice young woman came along and drove him out of the garage. Everything worked, his brakes, his engine, his bell, and they roared off up the quiet country road. They stopped at the nice woman's house and she brought out more toys than Number Nine had ever seen before.

There was a sandbox and building blocks, a slide and a painting table and books and dolls and a playhouse and jigsaws. There was even a tiny Number Nine bus. Then they drove to the nearest street and the children came running from their houses. They were the age that Number Nine liked the best. They were 3 and 4 and 5 years old. They all stopped in front of the Playbus. They touched its bright colours with their hands. They said, 'Did you ever see such a bus?' Then they rushed to get on it. Number Nine did not even mind when they pinged his bell all the time. All morning they

They said, 'Did you ever see such a bus?'

laughed and played with the toys. That night in his warm garage Number Nine said to himself:

'Oh, I'm so happy. I'm not getting old. I can hardly wait until the morning to get to play with all those children again.'

CALAMITY KATE AND THE RABBIT

Jennifer McCully

In one of the Marble Arch caves, near Lough
Erne in County Fermanagh, lived Calamity
Kate the witch. She wasn't a nasty horrible
witch who would put wicked spells on you, or
frighten you on a dark night. Calamity Kate was
the kindest, most well-meaning witch you
would meet in a day's walking.

The only trouble was, she had an awful habit
of getting her spells mixed up. It caused her all
sorts of bother, and that's why she was called
Calamity Kate.

Well, when our story begins poor Calamity
was feeling a bit down in the dumps as she
had just lost her faithful old black cat, Catkin
Purr. Perhaps 'lost' isn't quite the right word.
To tell the truth she had had an accident with

one of her spells and Catkin Purr had ended up as a bottle of black ink. Now it sat on a shelf in her cave, staring at her and making her feel terribly guilty. How she wished she could remember how to turn it back into a cat. In the meantime she was lonely. She needed someone to talk to, to sit on the end of her broomstick, to keep her company.

One evening she went out for a walk through the fields near her cave.

'Oh, how I *wish* I had something to talk to,' she said to herself. 'Something warm and furry, something cuddly, something …' She stopped. She could hardly believe her eyes – or her luck.

'Why, *there* it is. The very thing I've been looking for.'

What was it she had seen? Well, it was a very large and very furry rabbit sitting dozing peacefully under a lovely yellow whin bush. He had the most beautiful long ears which drooped down comfortably over his eyes and helped keep off the flies.

Calamity Kate tiptoed quietly up to him and gently picked up one of his long drooping ears.

'Hello ... PET,' she whispered into it.

The rabbit jumped up in a mixture of rage and fright and glared all round him.

'Here, clear off,' he shouted. '*Don't* touch my ears. And by the way, *what* did you call me just now?'

'I called you "Pet" of course,' answered Calamity, 'because after all you *are* goin' to be my new pet, and that *does* allow me to stroke your ears and ...'

'Your new WHAT?' shrieked the rabbit. His ears, which were his pride and joy quivered to their very tips. 'Who ever heard of a witch with a pet rabbit. Witches have black cats. And what's more, *no-one* is allowed to touch my ears.'

'A load of blethers,' shouted Calamity in excitement. 'Many's a rabbit would give his right ear just to be my pet. By the way, what's your name?'

'Flynn,' said the rabbit rather grandly, 'and if you think for one minute that *I'm* going to be *your* pet, or give you my right ear, you've got another th ...'

But he got no further. Calamity waved her hands in the air, there was a BANG and a WOOSH and before he knew what was happening Flynn found himself in the witch's cave.

'Now,' said Calamity, 'let's get sorted out. First we need to turn you black. So ...'

There was another BANG and WOOSH and Flynn was turned, not black but a sort of dirty pink with black splodges. All he could do was cry.

'Oops,' said Calamity. 'I must have got the spell wrong again. Ah well, never mind. You'll

Before he knew what was happening Flynn found himself in the witch's cave.

do very nicely like that. Now, I'll take you out for a bit of a run on the broomstick. That'll take your mind off it.'

'Oh no, no,' moaned Flynn. 'I hate flying – rabbits were never meant to fly. I'll be sick, I just know I will.'

'Quit bletherin',' said Calamity. 'Sure an outin' 'll do you good. Now, here goes.'

Before he could twitch a whisker Flynn found himself perched on the end of Calamity Kate's broomstick and they were zooming and diving over fields and hedges till he felt quite ill. He tried to squirm, to complain, to do anything that would make her stop, but it was no use.

'For dear sake, houl' your whisht and stop complainin',' she shouted as the wind whistled through Flynn's ears till he thought they were going to be blown off. After what seemed like ten years they got back to the cave.

'Now you'll be wantin' somethin' to eat,' said Calamity gaily, while Flynn collapsed in a corner. 'There, have some milk.' Flynn looked at it in horror. 'Don't be daft, I can't take that. Whoever heard of a rabbit drinking saucers of milk?'

'Oh, right enough, I never thought of that,' said Calamity.

'Tell you what, I was just about to put on a few spuds to make myself a good pot of champ. I'll put on some extra for you.'

'I can't eat champ,' wailed Flynn. 'What I need is carrots, lovely juicy carrots, and lettuce leaves and cabbage. I need something to *gnaw*.'

'Oh dear,' thought Calamity. 'I wonder if I've done the right thing with this rabbit business. I never had all this trouble feedin' my cats. And if only he wouldn't struggle so much when we're on the broomstick. Ach well, I'll just have to do my best to keep the poor wee thing happy.'

And so she did. She fitted a safety net below

*She fitted a safety net below the
broomstick in case he fell off.*

the broomstick in case he fell off; she got him a pair of goggles, to protect his eyes; she did everything any rabbit could want. But things didn't improve. If anything they got worse. Calamity came back to her cave one night to find Flynn busily gnawing the bristles off her broomstick.

'I *told* you I needed something to gnaw,' he said, when she screamed in horror. 'And anyway, I don't care about your broomstick, it's my ears I'm worried about. Sure last night didn't you use them as handlebars when we were out flying? They don't feel right yet.'

By now, Calamity was getting rather fed up with the whole thing. There was just no keeping Flynn happy.

'And what an appetite he has for all the size of him,' she thought.

The final straw came one cold November evening when they were out for a run on the broomstick. They were just crossing Lower Lough Erne when Calamity felt the broomstick starting to go down.

'*Now* what's happenin'?' she shouted. 'We're losin' height, we're goin' down, what's gone wrong? Oh no – the bristles are droppin' out of the broomstick – it's you, y'silly wee eejit, you've been gnawin' at them again, haven't you?'

It was true. Flynn, in his constant search for food had indeed been chewing the bristles off her broomstick. Down and down they came towards Lough Erne till finally they hit the icy water with a SPLASH. Somehow they struggled to dry land and made their way back to the cave.

'You were right all along,' said Calamity as they sat drying themselves by the fire. 'I've got to let you go. Rabbits were never meant to be witches' pets. First I must turn you back to your usual colour.' There was another BANG and more by good luck than anything else, Flynn found himself a grey rabbit once again.

'What happened to your last cat?' he asked, and sadly Calamity pointed to the little bottle of ink on the shelf.

'Oh, I see,' said Flynn, 'Tell you what, let's look through your spell book together and see if we can't get it sorted out.'

So that is what they did. There was another tremendous WOOSH and BANG, followed by – a little 'mew'.

'Catkin Purr!' shrieked Calamity in delight. She was so overjoyed to have her cat back again that she never even noticed as Flynn hopped off home to give his ears a good wash and brush and to have a good feed of carrots.

SCRUNCHY SIDEBOTTOM AND THE STONE MAN

Sam McAughtry

Glenda was sitting in the car, feeling a bit fed up.

Mummy had gone shopping and it was going to be a long wait.

Glenda sighed; the car was in the Square in Comber, beside a statue that rose high above everything else in town. On top of a tall pillar was the stone figure of a man, wearing tight trousers. A sword hung down by his side and his hand rested on the handle.

The stone man had been there for a hundred-and-forty-six years, so the people of Comber were used to it; they just walked past, and paid no attention to it at all.

Suddenly somebody rapped on the car window. Glenda looked out, and smiled all over

*It was Scrunchy Sidebottom, a magical friend,
who appeared at the most unexpected times.*

her face with delight; it was Scrunchy Sidebottom, a magical friend, who appeared at the most unexpected times.

He was dressed, as usual, in a green suit, and red pointy shoes; he had a long, pointy nose, and a red, pointy hat sat on top of his rather pointy head. As Scrunchy Sidebottom spoke, he was smiling too.

'I saw you looking up at the stone man, Glenda. I'm sure he's very pleased. Poor thing, nobody ever looks at him, you know.'

'Who on earth wants to look at an old stone man,' said Glenda. 'I was only doing it because I'm bored, and I've nothing else to do.'

'Well, it's not very nice to stand up fifty feet in the air and then have nobody look at you,' Scrunchy replied.

'Ah,' said Glenda, 'but that's because he's only an old stone man. If I stood on top of the pillar, or if you were up there, the whole town would look up.'

Scrunchy closed one eye in a long wink. 'You're about to find out; let's see if you're right; close your eyes, please.'

And Glenda closed her eyes and clapped her hands, for she knew that there was going to be a bit of magic.

Scrunchy took off his red pointy hat, closed his eyes, wrinkled his pointy nose, and sang:

Twinkle, twinkle, little star,
How I wonder where you are,
Are you high or are you low,
Or are you over Sandy Row?

When Glenda opened her eyes, Scrunchy Sidebottom had disappeared. She had a good idea where he had gone; she looked up.

Sure enough, Scrunchy was standing up in the stone man's place. He did look funny, with his pointy hat, and his pointy nose, and pretending to hold a sword by the handle.

Glenda looked around; not one person going past had noticed Scrunchy; they were all going about as if the stone man was still standing up on top of his pillar.

'There you are.' A strange voice made Glenda jump. 'Even when Scrunchy takes my place nobody notices him.'

Glenda nearly fell out of the car with surprise. It was the stone man, standing beside the car. Although he was a statue all over, he had a nice-looking, friendly face, and a bright smile. But quickly the smile faded; the stone man sighed.

'At least you looked at me, Glenda.'

Glenda didn't like to tell him that she had only looked at him because people always look up to the sky when they are bored. The stone man sighed again. 'I was a general in the army, you know. When I walked about, everybody would look at me; I even had friends who lived in Killyleagh Castle. But as soon as they made me a statue they all stopped looking. I've made up a rhyme about it. Would you like to hear it?'

Glenda loved rhymes; she nodded eagerly.

Up on my pillar, high in the air,
Nobody sees me in Comber Square.
Last time anyone said Hello
Was a hundred-and-forty-six years ago.

The stone man looked at the clock outside St Mary's Church hall. 'My goodness,' he said, 'I'll have to get back up there.' He shook hands with Glenda. 'Don't forget to look up at me now.' She could feel his hard, stone hand. Then he vanished.

Scrunchy appeared beside the car again. 'There, now,' he said, 'see what I mean?'

She could feel his hard, stone hand.

'I do.' Glenda shook her head with surprise. 'Nobody looked up at you at all.'

'Ah well,' Scrunchy said, 'another adventure's over. Time for home. Close your eyes please.'

Glenda closed her eyes while Scrunchy sang the song:

Twinkle, twinkle, little star,
How I wonder where you are,
Are you up or are you down,
Or are you over Andersonstown?

When Glenda opened her eyes again Scrunchy had disappeared.

She saw her Mummy coming. Soon the car started up. Glenda waved goodbye to the stone man, and she felt sure that, high up on his pillar, the stone man smiled down at her.

'Who are you waving at?' her Mummy asked.

'A general in the army,' Glenda said.

She could see that her Mummy thought that she was joking, so she didn't bother to explain.

MR McGONAGALL'S PROBLEM

Ann Burnett

'Bother,' said Mr McGonagall, the inventor, looking in his fridge. 'I've run out of milk for my tea again.'

He put on his boots and his hat and coat, ready to walk the three miles into Strabane to the nearest shop.

'Bother,' he said again, when he looked out of his cottage window. 'It's raining.'

Taking his umbrella, he plodded down the long garden path to the road.

'Look at my grass,' he moaned. 'It needs cut again. It never stops growing.'

Mr McGonagall trudged the three miles into Strabane for his milk and trudged the three miles home again.

When he reached his cottage, he said crossly,

Mr McGonagall trudged the three miles into Strabane for his milk and trudged the three miles home again.

'That grass has grown another centimetre since I've been out. I'll have to cut it again.'

Mr McGonagall was very cross.

'I'm fed up with this. I haven't any time left for inventing things. I spend all my time fetching milk and cutting my grass.'

Then he had a bright idea.

'Why don't I invent a machine that will do it all for me. A machine to fetch my milk and cut my grass.'

So he set to work in his shed. He banged and hammered and drew plans and scratched his head till eventually one morning, he wheeled out a robot.

It was slightly smaller than Mr McGonagall and made of shiny metal. It had an aerial coming from its head and two half moon shapes which opened and closed for hands.

Mr McGonagall pressed a lever on his control panel and the robot moved forward.

'Good,' said Mr McGonagall.

He pressed another lever and the robot's arms moved up and down.

'That's it,' said Mr McGonagall.

He moved several levers and pressed various buttons while red and green lights flashed.

'That's the robot programmed,' said Mr McGonagall. 'Go and fetch my milk.'

The robot whirred and clicked and set off down the road.

Mr McGonagall clapped his hands gleefully and went back to his shed to work. A little while later, he went to see if the robot had returned. There was no sign of it. Mr McGonagall had to walk all the way to the shop for his milk. On the way back, he spotted the robot lying in a ditch. A red light winked and it gave a tired whirr.

'Tut tut,' he said, picking it up. 'I hope you can cut grass better than you can fetch milk.'

When he got home, Mr McGonagall oiled the robot's joints and checked its circuits.

'There's nothing wrong with you,' he said, bringing out the lawn-mower.

'Cut the grass,' he ordered the robot, and pressed a button.

The robot's lights flashed and it whirred and clicked as it tried to push the lawn-mower. Then it stopped.

'Go on,' urged Mr McGonagall, fiddling with the control panel. 'Get a move on.'

The robot whirred and clicked even louder and pushed even harder but the lawn-mower did not budge.

Mr McGonagall stamped his feet.

'Oh botheration!' he said. 'Now what am I going to do?'

A farmer in the next field had been watching him.

'Having a spot of trouble?' he asked.

The robot whirred and clicked even louder and pushed even harder but the lawn-mower did not budge.

Mr McGonagall told him how he had to fetch his milk and cut his grass and that did not leave much time for inventing things.

'Fetching milk and cutting grass,' mused the farmer. 'I'll have a think about that.'

And he went back to his farm.

Mr McGonagall went into his cottage and made a cup of tea.

A little while later, the farmer knocked at his door.

'I've solved your problem,' he said to Mr McGonagall. 'I have brought you a Comprehensive Omnipotent Workmate.'

'A what!' gasped Mr McGonagall.

'A Comprehensive Omnipotent Workmate,' the farmer repeated. 'Or C.O.W. for short.'

'A C.O.W.!' Mr McGonagall said eagerly. 'Let me see this magnificent machine.'

He followed the farmer outside. There stood a brown and white cow.

'Moo,' it said.

'A C.O.W.,' said the farmer. 'It will eat your grass and give you milk every day.'

'A cow!' Mr McGonagall laughed. 'What a clever idea! I wish I'd thought of that.'

So now Mr McGonagall can spend all day inventing things, while Mabel the cow keeps his grass short and gives lots of milk.

And the robot? It stands in the shed and just occasionally gives a little whirr and a click!

THE GIANT'S WIFE

retold by Felicity Hayes-McCoy

Long ago there was a giant called Fionn McCool, and Fionn McCool lived with his wife, Una, in a big house in the County Tyrone. Across the sea in Scotland there lived another giant, and he lived in a cave on the windy hillside and not in a house at all.

Now, Fionn McCool was a big giant. He was as tall as a ten-storey house and as wide as the side of a lorry. His head was the size of a cinema screen and his little toe was as big as a doorstep. And he could run a hundred miles without even getting puffed. Everyone in the neighbourhood used to boast about how big he was, so his fame soon spread through the four provinces of Ireland. And pretty soon it spread across the sea to Scotland as well.

One morning, Una found Fionn sitting at the kitchen table in front of his tub of porridge. He always had porridge for breakfast because there weren't any cornflakes in those days. Even if there had been, it would have taken twenty boxes to fill Fionn.

He wasn't eating breakfast. He was just sitting there gloomily, chewing his thumbs. Una was very surprised.

'What's the matter with you,' she said. 'Is the porridge lumpy?'

'No, it's grand,' said Fionn. 'But I've just had some news that's put me right off it.'

'What's that?' said Una.

Fionn asked her if she'd ever heard of the Scottish Giant.

'Of course I have,' said Una. 'I know all about him. He's a big, huge, fierce giant, even bigger than you are. And he's got wild, shaggy red hair and great, jagged, broken teeth and a big, knotted ash stick that's longer than a double decker bus.'

'But what's he got to do with your breakfast?' she asked.

'He's coming to bash me up,' wailed Fionn. 'He says he's fed up hearing about me.'

You see, the Scottish Giant had heard the people of Tyrone boasting about how big and strong Fionn was. So he'd decided to pay him a visit and see for himself.

'Well, that'll teach you not to go boasting about how big you are,' said Una.

'I don't,' said Fionn. 'Well, maybe I do a bit. But what am I going to do now?' he said. 'He'll be halfway here already.'

'Hold your whisht and have your breakfast,' said she. 'I'll think of something.'

And she did.

She left Fionn to light the fire and heat the oven, and off she went to the neighbour's house to borrow a griddle.

A griddle is a round, flat pan made of iron. People used them to bake bread over the fire.

Now, when Una had borrowed the biggest griddle she could find, she rushed back home to make some bread. But when her loaf was shaped she pulled it in half and hid the griddle inside the dough. Then she baked it in the oven. So when it came out it had the hardest centre of any loaf ever made.

Then she made several other loaves as well, delicious, ordinary loaves that were crusty outside and soft within.

And then she sat down by the fire to do some sewing.

When she was finished, she held up a giant nightdress and a baby's cap that she'd made out of a tablecloth. Then she dressed Fionn up as a baby and tucked him into a wicker basket by the fire.

'Yes,' she said, 'were you
looking for someone?'

Now, Fionn had no idea what she was up to. But he did what she told him and he kept his mouth shut. As soon as he was in the basket, there was a knock on the door. And there was the Scottish Giant with his big stick.

Una smiled at him and she rocked the basket with her toe.

'Yes,' she said, 'were you looking for someone?'

And he told her he was looking for Fionn McCool.

'I'm afraid he's out at the moment,' said Una. 'He's just gone to knock down the town at the end of the valley.'

The Giant was impressed.

'Maybe you'd like to sit down and wait?' said Una. 'He'll only be ten minutes. Will you have a cup of tea in your hand?'

The Scottish Giant said he'd be delighted. But he was a little worried because he didn't

And he shoved and he heaved and he hauled and he pushed until the house was turned right round.

think *he* could flatten a whole town in ten minutes. And it seemed that Fionn could. So maybe it wasn't going to be that easy to bash him up after all.

Una got up to put the kettle on the fire. Then she shook her head sadly.

'Would you look at that,' she said. 'The wind's in the west again. Now if only Fionn were here he'd turn the house around. As it is, the fire will smoke and we'll have smokey tea.'

She sighed and she looked at the Scottish Giant. And what could he do but offer to help?

So up he got and off he went outside. And he shoved and he heaved and he hauled and he pushed until the house was turned right round.

By this time he was really worried. It was awfully hard work turning that house. And Una had behaved as if Fionn did it easily. Meanwhile Fionn was shivering in his basket. You see, he'd never turned the house round in his life. He wouldn't have been strong enough.

As soon as the Giant sat down again, Una gave him his tea.

'Here's a new-made loaf to go with it,' she said. And she handed him the loaf with the griddle in it.

He took a big bite. Then his tooth hit the griddle with an awful crack and he let a roar out of him that shook the house from attic to cellar.

'What's the matter?' said Una.

'Glory be to God, ma'am,' said the Scottish Giant, 'that bread's like iron.'

'Nonsense,' said Una. 'I only made it this morning. Sure the baby could eat that and come to no harm.'

She turned away and crossed to the basket by the fire. Then she picked up one of the ordinary loaves and handed it to Fionn. And

Fionn ate the loaf in two bites.

The Scottish Giant couldn't believe his eyes. He rushed over to the basket and then jumped back in alarm.

'That's a grand big baby, ma'am,' he said nervously. 'What age is he?'

Una shook her head.

'Oh, it's nice of you to say so,' she said, 'but he's not big at all for six months. Sure, his Daddy's ashamed of the size he is.'

'And is that a bit of the Daddy's bread he's after chewing?' said the Giant.

'It is,' said Una. 'He's got a grand set of teeth in his head, thank God. Fionn had all his teeth at two weeks, of course, but this lad's not doing badly. Would you like to feel them?' And she took his hand and guided it into Fionn's mouth.

Well Fionn mightn't have been as clever as his wife but he wasn't a fool altogether. He knew what to do when he felt the Scottish Giant's hand between his teeth. He bit him. He bit him as hard and as long as he could. And he didn't stop till the Giant was howling for mercy.

Una let on to be horrified.

'Oh, God forgive you, you bold child,' she said. 'Is it biting the nice gentleman and he only trying to be friendly? Just wait till your Daddy gets home.'

But if that was the baby, the Scottish Giant wasn't waiting to see the Daddy. He was out of the house and away down the road before Una had finished speaking. And he didn't stop running till he was back in his own cave on the windy hillside in the north of Scotland.